William J. Johnston

Christmas evergreens

English and american poetry

William J. Johnston

Christmas evergreens
English and american poetry

ISBN/EAN: 9783741191978

Manufactured in Europe, USA, Canada, Australia, Japa

Cover: Foto ©Andreas Hilbeck / pixelio.de

Manufactured and distributed by brebook publishing software
(www.brebook.com)

William J. Johnston

Christmas evergreens

" For the moon never beams without bringing me dreams
Of the beautiful Annabel Lee "

Christmas Evergreens:

A COLLECTION OF CHOICE

ENGLISH AND AMERICAN POETRY,

SUITABLE FOR

A HANDSOME HOLIDAY PRESENT

ILLUSTRATED BY A

FRONTISPIECE AND FIFTY FINE ENGRAVINGS.

NEW YORK:

W. J. JOHNSTON, COMPILER AND PUBLISHER,

No. 11 FRANKFORT STREET.

1879.

The compiler and publisher of this little volume has endeavored, both in regard to contents, illustrations, and typographical appearance, to present in " CHRISTMAS EVERGREENS " a neat and tasteful book for a holiday present, entertaining, instructive, and of permanent interest, at a price very much lower than works of this character are usually sold. How far he has succeeded, he leaves to the reader to say.

Acknowledgments are due Messrs. Houghton, Osgood & Co., for permission to use Mr. Longfellow's " Paul Revere's Ride," of which they hold the copyright, and to Messrs. D. Appleton & Co., for the privilege of adding Mr. Bryant's " Snow Shower."

LIST OF AUTHORS.

HENRY WADSWORTH LONGFELLOW,
WILLIAM CULLEN BRYANT,
JAMES MONTGOMERY,
WILLIAM WORDSWORTH,
ALFRED TENNYSON,
SIR HENRY WOTTON,
BENJAMIN F. TAYLOR,
GEORGE T. LANIGAN,
OLIVER GOLDSMITH,
SARAH E. HENSHAW,
I. McLELLAN, JR.,
WILLIAM KNOX,
MEDORA CLARK,
THOMAS GRAY,
A. C. BOLTON,
J. C. SHERER,
JANE TAYLOR,
ELIZA COOK,
E. TAYLOR.

PAUL REVERE'S RIDE.

THE LANDLORD'S TALE.

ISTEN, my children, and you shall hear
Of the midnight ride of Paul Revere,
On the eighteenth of April, in Seventy-five;
Hardly a man is now alive
Who remembers that famous day and year.

He said to his friend : "If the British march
By land or sea from the town to-night,
Hang a lantern aloft in the belfry arch
Of the North Church tower as a signal light,—
One, if by land, and two, if by sea ;
And I on the opposite shore will be,
Ready to ride and spread the alarm

Through every Middlesex village and farm,
For the country-folk to be up and to arm."

Then he said "Good night!" and with muffled
Silently rowed to the Charlestown shore,
Just as the moon rose over the bay,
Where, swinging wide at her moorings, lay
The Somerset, British man-of-war,—
A phantom-ship, with each mast and spar
Across the moon like a prison bar,
And a huge black hulk that was magnified
By its own reflection in the tide.

Meanwhile his friend, through alley and street,
Wanders and watches with eager ears,
Till in the silence around him he hears
The muster of men at the barrack door,

The sound of arms and the tramp of feet,
And the measured tread of the grenadiers
Marching down to their boats on the shore.

hen he climbed the tower of the Old North Church,
y the wooden stairs, with stealthy tread,
o the belfry-chamber overhead,
nd startled the pigeons from their perch
n the sombre rafters, that round him made
Iasses and moving shapes of shade,---
y the trembling ladder, steep and tall,
o the highest window in the wall,
Vhere he paused to listen and look down
moment on the roofs of the town,
nd the moonlight flowing over all.

Beneath, in the churchyard, lay the dead,
In their night-encampment on the hill,

Wrapped in silence so deep and still
That he could hear, like a sentinel's tread,
The watchful night-wind, as it went
Creeping along from tent to tent,
And seeming to whisper: "All is well!"
A moment only he feels the spell
Of the place and the hour, and the secret dread
Of the lonely belfry and the dead ;
For suddenly all his thoughts are bent
On a shadowy something far away,
Where the river widens to meet the bay,--
A line of black that bends and floats
On the rising tide, like a bridge of boats.

Meanwhile, impatient to mount and ride,
Booted and spurred, with a heavy stride
On the opposite shore walked Paul Revere.
Now he patted his horse's side,
Now gazed at the landscape far and near,
Then, impetuous, stamped the earth,
And turned and tightened his saddle-girth ;
But mostly he watched with eager search
The belfry tower of the Old North Church,
As it rose above the graves on the hill,
Lonely and spectral and sombre and still.
And lo ! as he looks, on the belfry's height
A glimmer, and then a gleam of light !
He springs to the saddle, the bridle he turns,

But lingers and gazes, till full on his sight
A second lamp in the belfry burns !

A hurry of hoofs in a village street,
A shape in the moonlight, a bulk in the dark,
And beneath, from the pebbles in passing, a spark
Struck out by a steed flying fearless and fleet :
That was all ! And yet, through the gloom and the light,
The fate of a nation was riding that night :

And the spark struck out by that steed in his flight
Kindled the land into flame with its heat.

He has left the village and mounted the steep,
And beneath him, tranquil and broad and deep,
Is the Mystic, meeting the ocean tides :
And under the alders that skirt its edge,
Now soft on the sand, now loud on the ledge,
Is heard the tramp of his steed as he rides.

It was twelve by the village clock
When he crossed the bridge into Medford town.
He heard the crowing of the cock,
And the barking of the farmer's dog,
And felt the damp of the river fog,
That rises after the sun goes down.

It was one by the village clock
When he galloped into Lexington.
He saw the gilded weathercock
Swim in the moonlight as he passed,
And the meeting-house windows, blank and bare,
Gaze at him with a spectral glare,
As if they already stood aghast
At the bloody work they would look upon.

It was two by the village clock
When he came to the bridge in Concord town.
He heard the bleating of the flock,
And the twitter of birds among the trees,
And felt the breath of the morning breeze
Blowing over the meadows brown.
And one was safe and asleep in his bed
Who at the bridge would be first to fall,—
Who that day would be lying dead,
Pierced by a British musket-ball.

You know the rest. In the books you have read
How the British Regulars fired and fled,—

How the farmers gave them ball for ball,
From behind each fence and farm-yard wall,

Chasing the red-coats down the lane,
Then crossing the fields to emerge again
Under the trees at the turn of the road,
And only pausing to fire and load.
So through the night rode Paul Revere ;
And so through the night went his cry of alarm
To every Middlesex village and farm.—
A cry of defiance and not of fear,
A voice in the darkness, a knock at the door,
And a word that shall echo forevermore !
For, borne on the night-wind of the Past,
Through all our history to the last,
In the hour of darkness and peril and need,
The people will waken and listen to hear
The hurrying hoof-beats of that steed.
And the midnight message of Paul Revere.

THE NOTES OF THE BIRDS.

ELL do I love those various harmonies
That ring so gaily in spring's budding
woods,
And in the thickets, and green, quiet haunts,
And lovely copses of the summer-time,
And the red autumn's ancient solitudes.

How rich the varied choir! The unquiet finch
Calls from the distant hollows, and the wren
Uttereth her sweet and mellow plaint at times,
And the thrush mourneth where the kalmia hangs
In crimson spotted cups, or chirps, half hid,
Amid the lowly dogwood's snowy flowers.

In the last days of autumn, when the corn
Lies sweet and yellow in the harvest field,
And the gay company of reapers bind
The bearded wheat in sheaves,—then peals abroad
The blackbird's merry chant. I love to hear,
Bold plunderer, thy mellow burst of song
Float from thy watch-place on the mossy tree,
Close at the corn-field edge.

THE SWAN.

BEHOLD! the mantling spirit of reserve
Fashions his neck into a goodly curve,
An arch thrown back between luxuriant
    wings
  Of whitest garniture, like fir-tree boughs,
To which, on some unruffled morning,
    clings
  A flaky weight of winter's purest snow.

THE CHRISTMAS TREE.

H, the Christmas tree! the Christmas tree!
  Green are the boughs of the Christmas tree;
And wherever I am, on the land or the sea,
There always appears at this season to me
The vision bright of a Christmas tree.

I have been in lands where ice and snow
Were all around, above and below;
But even then I caught the glow,
Shimmering over a wintry sea.
From a distant land and the Christmas tree.

In lands that are scorched by a tropical sun,
Where summer and winter are both as one,

I have stood on the shore when the day was done,
And caught the echoes of innocent glee
From a far-away land and a Christmas tree.

Wherever I am, in the East or the West,
Though distant from home and the ones I love best,
I feel that I am by its memories blest;
And over the miles intervening I see
The glimmering light of the Christmas tree.

Let the voices of sorrow and mourning cease,
And the mourner break forth in a carol of peace;
And over each care, like a golden fleece,
Fall the halo of love, with its benison free,
On the hearts that are cheered by the Christmas tree.

Away with all doubts, all cares and fears,—
It is not the season for sighs and tears;
For down through the eighteen hundred years
Comes a voice that is saying to you and to me:
"Rejoice, for I gave you the Christmas tree."

Brightly the stars may be shining to-night,
The moon flood the world with its silvery light,
Or the clouds hide the moon and the stars from our sight;
But we care not how heavy the darkness may be,
There's no cloud o'er the light of the Christmas tree!

There are gifts here for all, for the young and the old ;
Here are trinkets and toys of more value than gold :
May the warm hearts that proffer them never grow cold,
But look back, from the heights of the future to be,
At the bright shining lights of this Christmas tree.

Oh, the Christmas tree ! the Christmas tree !
'Tis a beautiful sight for the eye to see
The cheerful wave of its branches green,
And friendship's gifts that are placed between :
Oh, a beautiful sight is the Christmas tree !

IN PRAISE OF ANGLING.

ABUSED mortals! did you know
Where joy, heart's ease and comforts
    grow,
    You'd scorn proud towers
    And seek them in these bowers.
Where winds sometimes our woods,
    perhaps, may shake,
But blustering care could never tempest make.

    Blest silent groves, O, may you be
    Forever mirth's best nursery!
      May pure contents
      Forever pitch their tents
Upon these downs, these meads, rocks and mountains,
And peace still slumber by these purling fountains.

THE HORSE.

HE Horse! the brave, the gallant Horse—
Fit theme for the minstrel's song!
He hath good claim to praise and fame,
As the fleet, the kind, the strong.

Behold him free in his native strength,
Looking fit for the sun-god's car;
With a skin as sleek as a maiden's cheek,
And an eye like the Polar star.

Who wonders not such limbs can deign
To brook the fettering girth;
As we see him fly the ringing plain,
And paw the crumbling earth?

His nostrils are wide with snorting pride,
   His fiery veins expand ;
And yet he'll be led by a silken thread,
   Or soothed by an infant's hand.

He ownes the lion's spirit and might,
   But the voice he has learnt to love
Needs only be heard, and he'll turn to the word,
   As gentle as a dove.

A song for the steed, the gallant steed—
   Oh ! grant him a leaf of bay ;
For we owe much more to his strength and speed
   Than man can ever repay.

Whatever his place—the yoke, the chase,
   The war-field, road, or course,
One of Creation's highest and best
   Is the Horse, the noble Horse !

THE SNOW SHOWER.

STAND here by my side and turn, I pray,
  On the lake below thy gentle eyes;
The clouds hang over it heavy and gray,
  And dark and silent the water lies;
And out of that frozen mist the snow
  In wavering flakes begins to flow:
        Flake after flake
  They sink in the dark and silent lake.

See how in a living swarm they come
  From the chambers beyond that misty vail;
Some hover awhile in air, and some
  Rush prone from the sky like summer hail.

All, dropping swiftly or settling slow,
  Meet, and are still in the depths below:
      Flake after flake
  Dissolved in the dark and silent lake.

Here delicate snow-stars, out of the cloud,
  Come floating downward in airy play,
Like spangles dropped from the glistening crowd
  That whiten by night the milky way;
There broader and burlier masses fall;
  The sullen water buries them all—
      Flake after flake—
  All drowned in the dark and silent lake.

And some, as on tender wings they glide,
  From their chilly birth-cloud, dim and gray,
Are joined in their fall, and, side by side,
  Come clinging along their unsteady way;
As friend with friend, or husband with wife,
  Makes hand in hand the passage of life:
      Each mated flake
  Soon sinks in the dark and silent lake.

Lo! while we are gazing, in swifter haste
  Stream down the snows, till the air is white,
As, myriads by myriads madly chased,
  They fling themselves from their shadowy height:

The fair, frail creatures of middle sky,
  What speed they make, with their grave so nigh ;
        Flake after flake,
  To lie in the dark and silent lake !

I see in thy gentle eyes a tear ;
  They turn to me in sorrowful thought ;
Thou thinkest of friends, the good and dear,
  Who were for a time, and now are not ;
Like these fair children of cloud and frost,
  That glisten a moment and then are lost,
        Flake after flake—
All lost in the dark and silent lake.

Yet look again, for the clouds divide ;
  A gleam of blue on the water lies ;
And far away, on the mountain side,
  A sunbeam falls from the opening skies.
But the hurrying host that flew between
  The cloud and the water, no more is seen :
        Flake after flake
  At rest in the dark and silent lake.

THE TELEGRAM.

DEAD, did you say? he! dead in his prime!
Son of my mother! my brother! my friend!
While the horologe points to the noon of his time,
Has his sun set in darkness? is all at an end?

("*By a sudden accident,*")

Dead! it is not, it cannot, it must not be true!
Let me read the dire words for myself, if I can;
Relentless, hard, cold they rise on my view—
They blind me! how did you say that they ran?

("*He was mortally injured,*")

Dead ! around me I hear the singing of birds,
  And the breath of June roses comes in at the pane ;
Nothing—nothing is changed by those terrible words ;
  They cannot be true ! let me see them again !

  (" *And died yesterday*,")

Dead ! a letter but yesterday told of his love !
  Another to-morrow the tale will repeat ;
Outstripped by this thunderbolt flung from above,
  Scathing my heart, as it falls at my feet !

  (" *Funeral to-morrow*,")

Oh ! terrible Telegraph ! subtle and still !
  Darting thy lightnings with pitiless haste !
No kind warning thunder — no storm-boding thrill—
  But one fierce deadly flash, and the heart lieth waste !

  (" *Inform his friends*.")

TO A BUTTERFLY.

MUCH converse do I find in thee,
　Historian of my infancy !
　　Float near me; do not yet depart,
　　Dead times revive in thee :
　　Thou bringest, gay creature as thou art,
　　A solemn image to my heart,
　　My father's family !
　　Oh pleasant, pleasant were the days,
　　The time when, in our childish plays,
　　My sister Emmeline and I
　　Together chased the butterfly !
　　A very hunter did I rush
　　Upon the prey with leaps and springs,
　　But she—God love her ! feared to brush
　　The dust from off its wings.

LULLABY.

SWEET and low, sweet and low,
    Wind of the western sea,
  Over the rolling waters go,
  Come from the dying moon and blow,
    Blow him again to me,
  While my little one, while my pretty one,
      sleeps.
Sleep and rest, on mother's breast,
  Father will come to thee soon,
  Father will come to his babe in the nest,
  Silver sails all out of the west,
      Under the silver moon.
  Sleep, my little one, sleep, my pretty one, sleep.

PROFESSOR MORSE.*

Dids't thou die to be at rest,
Thou of the noble soul and giant mind?
Had'st thou grown weary in the hopeless quest
Of blessedness that mortals seldom find?
Had care and toil and sorrow all combined
To bring that sickness of soul, that mars
The happiness that God for men designed,

---

* This poem was suggested by the remark once made by Professor Morse to
a friend: "I would gladly have availed myself of any divine authorization to
terminate a life of which the possessor was weary."

Till thy sad spirit spurned its prison bars,
  And pined to soar away amid the burning stars.

Perchance an angel sought thee in that hour,
  A blessed angel from the world of light,
Teaching submission to Almighty power,
  Whose dealings all are equal, just, and right.
Perchance Hope whispered of a future, bright
  And glorious in its triumphs.   Soon it came.
A world admiring hailed thee with delight,
  And learned joyed to trace thy deathless name
  Upon her ponderous tomes in characters of flame.

Thou brightest meteor of a starry age,
  What does the world not owe thee ?
Thou hast wrought for scientific lore a glowing page,
  Thy mighty energy of mind has brought
To man a wondrous agent ; it has taught
  The viewless lightning, in flight sublime,
To bear upon its wings embodied thought,
  Warm from its birth-place to the farthest clime,
  Annihilating space, vanquishing e'en time.

Did'st thou look down into the shadowy tomb,
  And crave the privilege to slumber there,
Unhonored and forgotten ?   Thou on whom
  Kind heaven bestowed endowments rich and rare,
Was life a burden that thou could'st not bear ?

A lesson this to those whose souls have striven
With disappointment, sorrow, and despair,
   Until they feed on poison, and are driven
   To quench the vital spark that Deity hath given.

And it should teach our restless hearts how dim
   And erring is our finite vision here, —
Should make us trust, through humble faith, in Him
   Who sees alike the distant and the near.
When storm clouds gather o'er us dark and drear,
   And lightnings flash, and winds are wild and high,
No radiant beam of sunshine comes to cheer;
   But when the wrecking tempest has gone by,
   God sets the blessed bow of promise in the sky.

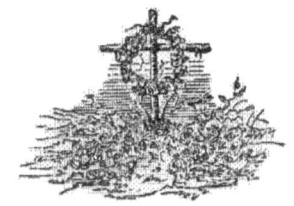

CHRISTMAS TIDE.

WHEN the merry Spring-time weaves
Its peeping bloom and dewy leaves;
When the primrose opes its eye,
And the young moth flutters by;
When the plaintive turtle dove
Pours its notes of peace and love;
And the clear sun flings its glory bright and wide.
Yet, yet my soul will own
More joy in Winter's frown,
And wake with warmer flush at Christmas tide.

The summer beams may shine
On the rich and curling vine,
And the noontide rays light up
The tulip's dazzling cup;

But the pearly mistletoe
And the holly-berries' glow
Are not even by the boasted rose outvied ;
For the happy hearts beneath
The green and coral wreath
Love the garlands that are twined at Christmas tide.

Let the Autumn days produce
Yellow corn and purple juice,
And Nature's feast be spread
In the fruitage ripe and red ;
'Tis grateful to behold
Gushing grapes and fields of gold,
When cheeks are brown'd and rich lips deeper dyed ;
But give, oh ! give to me
The Winter night of glee,
The mirth and plenty seen at Christmas tide.

The northern gust may howl,
The rolling storm-cloud scowl,
King Frost may make a slave
Of the river's rapid wave,
The snow-drift choke the path,
Or the hail-shower spend its wrath ;
But the sternest blast right bravely is defied ;
While limbs and spirits bound
To the merry minstrel sound,
And social wood-fires blaze at Christmas tide.

The song, the laugh, the shout,
Shall mock the storm without ;
And sparkling wine-foam rise
'Neath still more sparkling eyes ;
The forms that rarely meet,
Then hand to hand shall greet,
And soul pledge soul that leagues too long divide :
Mirth, Friendship, Love, and Light,
Shall crown the Winter night,
And every glad voice welcome Christmas tide.

But while Joy's echo falls
In gay and plenteous halls,
Let the poor and lowly share
The warmth, the sports, the fare ;
For the one of humble lot
Must not shiver in his cot,
But claim a bounteous meed from Wealth and Pride :
Shed kindly blessings round,
Till no aching heart be found ;
And then all hail to merry Christmas tide !

THE BUTTERFLY.

HE butterfly, an idle thing,
Nor honey makes, nor yet can sing,
   As do the bee and bird ;
Nor does it, like the prudent ant,
Lay up of grain, for time of want,
   A wise and cautious hoard.

My youth is but a summer's day :
Then, like the bee and ant, I'll lay
   A store of learning by ;
And though from flower to flower I rove,
My stock of wisdom I'll improve,
   Nor be a butterfly.

HOME.

THERE is a land, of every land the pride,
Beloved by Heaven o'er all the world beside;
Where brighter suns dispense serener light,
And milder moons emparadise the night;
A land of beauty, virtue, valor, truth,
Time-tutored age, and love-exalted youth:
The wandering mariner, whose eye explores
The wealthiest isles, the most enchanting shores,
Views not a realm so bountiful and fair,
Nor breathes the spirit of a purer air;
In every clime the magnet of his soul,
Touched by remembrance, trembles to that pole;

For in this land of Heaven's peculiar grace,
The heritage of nature's noblest race,
There is a spot of earth supremely blest—
A dearer, sweeter spot than all the rest—
Where man, creation's tyrant, casts aside
His sword and sceptre, pageantry and pride,
While in his softened looks benignly blend
The sire, the son, the husband, brother, friend.
Here woman reigns ; the mother, daughter, wife,
Strew with fresh flowers the narrow way of life :
In the clear heaven of her delightful eye
An angel-guard of loves and graces lie ;
Around her knees domestic duties meet,
And fireside pleasures gambol at her feet.
"Where shall that land, that spot of earth be found ?"
Art thou a man?—a patriot?—look around ;
Oh, thou shalt find, howe'er thy footsteps roam,
That land thy country, and that spot thy home.

. . . .

Man, through all ages of revolving time,
Unchanging man, in every varying clime,
Deems his own land of every land the pride,
Beloved of Heaven o'er all the world beside ;
His home the spot of earth supremely blest,
A dearer, sweeter spot than all the rest.

SONG FOR THE SPINNING WHEEL.

Softly turn the murmuring wheel!
 Night has brought the welcome hour,
When the weary fingers feel
 Help, as if from fairy power;
Dewy night o'ershades the ground:
Turn the swift wheel round and round!

Short-lived likings may be bred
 By a glance from fickle eyes,
But true love is like the thread
 Which the kindly wool supplies,
While the flock are all at rest,
Sleeping on the mountain's breast.

FATE.

As two proud ships upon the pathless main
Meet once, and never hope to meet again,—
Meet once, with merry signalings, and part,
Each homeward bound to swell the crowded
    mart,
So we two met, one golden summer day,
Within the shelter of Life's dreaming bay,
And rested, calmly anchored from the world,
For one brief hour, with snowy pinions furled,
But when the sun sank low along the west,
We left our harbor, with its peaceful rest,
And floated outward on Life's tangled sea,
With foam-kissed waves between us, wild and
    free,
As two ships part upon the trackless main,
So we two parted. Shall we meet again?

O! WHY SHOULD THE SPIRIT OF MORTAL BE PROUD ?

why should the spirit of mortal be proud ?
Like a swift-fleeting meteor, a fast-flying cloud,
A flash of the lightning, a break of the wave,
Man passes from life to his rest in the grave.

The leaves of the oak and the willow shall fade,
Be scattered around and together be laid ;
And the young and the old, and the low and the high,
Shall moulder to dust and together shall lie.

The infant a mother attended and loved,
The mother that infant's affection who proved :

The husband that mother and infant who blessed,
Each, all, are away to their dwellings of rest.

The maid on whose cheek, on whose brow, in whose eye,
Shone beauty and pleasure,—her triumphs are by ;
And the memory of those who loved her and praised,
Are alike from the minds of the living erased.

The hand of the king that the sceptre hath borne,
The brow of the priest that the mitre hath worn ;
The eye of the sage and the heart of the brave,
Are hidden and lost in the depth of the grave.

The peasant, whose lot was to sow and to reap;
The herdsman, who climbed with his goats up the steep ;
The beggar, who wandered in search of his bread,
Have faded away like the grass that we tread.

The saint who enjoyed the communion of heaven ;
The sinner who dared to remain unforgiven ;
The wise and the foolish, the guilty and just,
Have quietly mingled their bones in the dust.

So the multitude goes, like the flower or the weed
That withers away to let others succeed ;
So the multitude comes, even those we behold,
To repeat every tale that has often been told.

For we are the same our fathers have been ;
We see the same sights our fathers have seen ;
We drink the same stream and view the same sun,
And run the same course our fathers have run.

The thoughts we are thinking our fathers would think,
From the death we are shrinking our fathers would shrink,
To the life we are clinging they also would cling ;
But it speeds for us all, like a bird on the wing.

They loved, but the story we cannot unfold ;
They scorned, but the heart of the haughty is cold,
They grieved, but no wail from their slumber will come;
They joyed, but the tongue of their gladness is dumb.

They died, aye ! they died ; and we things that are now,
Who walk on the turf that lies over their brow,
Who make in their dwelling a transient abode,
Meet the things that they met on their pilgrimage road.

Yea ! hope and despondency, pleasure and pain,
We mingle together in sunshine and rain ;
And the smiles and the tears, the song and the dirge,
Still follow each other, like surge upon surge.

'Tis the wink of an eye, 'tis the draught of a breath,
From the blossom of health to the paleness of death,
From the gilded saloon to the bier and the shroud—
O, why should the spirit of mortal be proud ?

EVENING.

ITTLE girl, it is time to retire to your rest,
   The sheep are put into the fold,
The linnet forsakes us, and flies to her nest,
   To shelter her young from the cold.

The owl has flown out of his lonely retreat,
   And screams through the tall shady trees :
The nightingale takes on the hawthorn her seat,
   And sings to the soft dying breeze.

The sun appears now to have finish'd his race,
   And sinks once again to his rest ;
But though we no longer can see his bright face,
   He leaves a gold streak in the west.

SPRING.

o ! where the rosy-bosomed Hours,
   Fair Venus' train, appear,
Disclose the long-expecting flowers
   And wake the purple year !
The Attic warbler pours her throat
Responsive to the cuckoo's note,
   The untaught harmony of spring :
While, whispering pleasures as they fly,
Cool zephyrs through the clear blue sky
   Their gathered fragrance fling.

Where'er the oak's thick branches stretch
  A broader, browner shade,
Where'er the rude and moss-grown beech
  O'er-canopies the glade,
Beside some water's rushy brink
With me the Muse shall sit, and think
  (At ease reclined in rustic state)
How vain the ardor of the crowd,
How low, how little are the proud,
  How indigent the great!

Still is the toiling hand of care;
  The panting herds repose:
Yet hark, how through the peopled air
  The busy murmur glows!
The insect youth are on the wing,
Eager to taste the honeyed spring
  And float amid the liquid noon:
Some lightly o'er the current skim,
Some show their gayly gilded trim
  Quick-glancing to the sun.

To Contemplation's sober eye
  Such is the race of man;
And they that creep, and they that fly
  Shall end where they began.

Alike the busy and the gay
But flutter through life's little day,
    In Fortune's varying colors drest :
Brushed by the hand of rough mischance
Or chilled by age, their airy dance
    They leave, in dust to rest.

Methinks I hear in accents low
    The sportive kind reply :
    Poor moralist ! and what art thou ?
        A solitary fly !
Thy joys no glittering female meets,
No hive hast thou of hoarded sweets,
    No painted plumage to display ;
On hasty wings thy youth is flown ;
Thy sun is set, thy spring is gone,—
    We frolic while 'tis May.

THE TELEPHONE.

HE world stood still for a thousand years,
    And crept for a thousand more,
This wonderful world with wings for ears,
    Like the Messenger god of yore—
And winged feet and winged wand,
    And a wing on its either hand,
And more than Mercury wore.

It bridles and rides a furnace's foal,
    With iron and hammer for sire,
Great clouds of white from their nostrils roll,
    And it feeds its horses fire!
They are blooded stock, the engines swift:
    Beneath their heels the distances drift
Like snows from the Arctic Pole!

They rattle across the meridian lines,
  And down the parallels play ;
They marry together the palms and pines,

  A thousand miles in a day.
The world has trained a wonderful wire,
A nerve of a route for articulate fire,
  And taught the lightnings to say :

"Dear Mary, be mine!"—"Car-load of swine"—
"One ton of cheese"—"Maria dead"—
"Joy! it's a boy!"—"I'm coming to dine"—

"Send soap"—"She's married to Fred."
The humblest of words like angels fly
A thousand miles in the flash of an eye.
You hear before they are said!

What happened at ten you know at nine,
  And you away in the West,
They distance along the lightning line
  The sun in his golden rest ;
They talk to-day in audible tone,
The telegraph turns the telephone,
  And parted lovers are blest !

Think of a girl in a lonely hour,
  No beau in forty miles,
She sits by the tube of talking power,
  She thinks a minute, and smiles.
"I'll call my John," you fancy her say,
"He lives but a hundred miles away,
  And banish the weary wiles."

Behold them at the ends of the line,
  This John and his black-eyed boon ;
His head and her's to the wire incline,
  And she sings him Bonny Doon.
He sighs for the only thing amiss,
He has no voice, but then he can—kiss !
  He might as well be in the moon !
For emptier than an east wind's laugh
Is a lover's kiss by telegraph !

THE TELEGRAPH WIRES.

THE WIRES LOQUENTUR.

URRAH for the veins of the country,
  Throbbing with fiery blood !
Hurrah for the wires that carry the thoughts
  Of the city's multitude !

The gleaming rails are the sinews
  That sway the strong right hand,
But the wires carry the heart-blood thoughts
  Across the busy land.

Hurrah for the purple prairies
That robe our royal land !
Hurrah for the dark green glory of pines
That tower on every hand !
And hurrah for the father of harvests
That gallops to meet the sea,
As a warrior spurs a foaming steed
To the perilous victory !

We're at home in the pathless prairie ;
We're at home in the solemn woods,

Where the red fox patters over red leaves,
And whirs the partridge brood.
Then away across the sunset land,
By homesteads mossed and gray,

The march of the lessening telegraph wires
　　Goes into the reddened day.

Deep down in the silent water,
　　Where a tremulous splendor dwells,
On the slanting walls of golden halls
　　And the rainbows of the shells,
Our wires are speaking living words ;
　　Down in the dusky gloom
Clicking away, night and day ;
　　Passionless tongue that never tires.
Joy and grief have a similar sound
　　Over the wires.

THE WIRES IN PEACE.

We start from the busy city,
　　That throbs to the rush of feet,

Where the hurrying army of trade
  Goes rushing down the street.

We pass the white-walled cottages,
  Where the pleasant sound of bees
Crones the sultry day to sleep
  In the clover under the trees.

The iron horse flings his smoky mane,
  As he thunders among the hills,
Shaking the harvest fields that dance
  To a murmur of musical rills.
We cling to his trail in the happy land ;
  We bend above the stream ;
And our glimmering posts troop by like ghosts
  In the traveler's midnight dream.

THE WIRES IN WAR.

We march in the van of the army
That rolls to the far-away fight,
And our banners glow with the presence
Of the God who strikes for the right—

Past the pickets that sternly stand
Each on his lonely post,

While the moonbeam shimmers on the tents
  Above the sleeping host.

We see them march to the battle,
  And our veins are big with pride.

When the blue coats stoop to the shower of lead
  That rains from the mountain side ;
Till the battle is white with smoke ;
  And over the wild unrest
Stream in fierce joy the burning stars
  Of the land we love the best.

We hurry, hurry homeward,
  When the long day's battle is done.

With news of a great one fallen—
    With news of a great fight won.
We thrill along the endless words,
    We sing by lowly eaves,
Where the birds fly like a flash of light
    Amid the dark cool leaves.

Where women watch with weary eyes,
    And little children wait,
Under the musical sycamore
    Down by the garden gate ;
And down in the office, from white lips
    Faint breath comes quick and short
When the sounder clicks the list of killed
    In the afternoon report.

THE WIRES IN THE CITY.

We leave the cottage home behind ;
　A gloomy sunset steals
Over the city where the streets
　Are thunderous with wheels.
Busy all day the key has been ;
　Busy all night the types shall be ;
To-morrow the news is in the land
　Of a glorious victory !

Crowds are choking every street,
　And great bells boom in stately towers ;
Flags flutter out on smoky roofs—
　After the battle, joy is ours ;
Joy on the land, joy on the lake,
　Where a hundred ripples of sunshine laugh,

And joy where the ragged newsboy shouts :
"Great news by telegraph ! "

THE WIRES UNIVERSALLY.

We bring glad news to inland homes
    Of ships upon the sea ;
We hurry along the murderer's trail—
    His Nemesis are we.

We watch all night the roaring trains,
    When the sleepless sounder clicks
A caution for Number Seven past
    To wait for Number Six.
We are knitting land to brother land,
    And hurrying on the day
When the clouds about the glorious stars
    Shall all be rolled away ;
When the people shall learn war no more,
    Nor again the cymbal clash,
And all the nations speak one speech—
    The telegraph dot and dash.

THE NIGHTINGALE.

Thy plaintive notes, sweet Philomel,
All other melodies excel :
  Deep in the grove retired.
Thou seem'st thyself and song to hide.
Nor dost thou boast, or plume with pride,
  Nor wish to be admired.

So, if endued with power and grace,
And with that power my will keep pace,
  I'll act a generous part :
And banish ostentatious show,
Nor let my liberal action know
  A witness but my heart.

THE DESERTED VILLAGE.

SWEET Auburn! loveliest village of
    the plain,
Where health and plenty cheered the laboring swain,
Where smiling spring its earliest visit paid,
And parting summer's lingering blooms delayed.
Dear lovely bowers of innocence and ease,
Seats of my youth, when every sport could please,
How often have I loitered o'er thy green,
Where humble happiness endeared each scene!
How often have I paused on every charm,
The sheltered cot, the cultivated farm,

The never-failing brook, the busy mill,
The decent church that topped the neighboring hill,
The hawthorn bush, with seats beneath the shade,
For talking age and whispering lovers made !
How often have I blessed the coming day,
When toil remitting lent its turn to play,
And all the village train, from labor free,
Led up their sports beneath the spreading tree,
While many a pastime circled in the shade,
The young contending as the old surveyed :
And many a gambol frolicked o' er the ground,
And sleights of art and feats of strength went round;
And still as each repeated pleasure tired,
Succeeding sports the mirthful band inspired ;
The dancing pair that simply sought renown,
By holding out, to tire each other down ;
The swain mistrustless of his smutted face,
While secret laughter tittered round the place ;
The bashful virgin's sidelong looks of love,
The matron's glance that would those looks reprove,
These were thy charms, sweet village ! sports like these
With sweet succession, taught e'en toil to please ;
These round thy bowers their cheerful influence shed,
These were thy charms,—but all these charms are fled,
     Sweet smiling village, loveliest of the lawn,
Thy sports are fled, and all thy charms withdrawn ;

Amidst thy bowers the tyrant's hand is seen,
And desolation saddens all thy green;
One only master grasps the whole domain,
And half a tillage stints thy smiling plain;
No more thy glassy brook reflects the day,
But, chok'd with sedges, works its weedy way;
Along thy glades, a solitary guest,
The hollow-sounding bittern guards its nest;
Amidst thy desert walks the lapwing flies,
And tires their echoes with unvaried cries.
Sunk are thy bowers in shapeless ruin all,
And the long grass o'ertops the mouldering wall,

And trembling, shrinking from the spoiler's hand,
Far, far away thy children leave the land.

Ill fares the land, to hastening ills a prey,
Where wealth accumulates, and men decay:
Princes and lords may flourish, or may fade;
A breath can make them, as a breath has made;
But a bold peasantry, their country's pride,
When once destroyed, can never be supplied.

A time there was, ere England's griefs began,
When every rood of ground maintained its man;
For him light labor spread her wholesome store,
Just gave what life required, but gave no more;
His best companions, innocence and health;
And his best riches, ignorance of wealth.

But times are altered; trade's unfeeling train
Usurp the land and dispossess the swain;
Along the lawn, where scattered hamlets rose,
Unwieldy wealth and cumberous pomp repose;

And every want to luxury allied,
And every pang that folly pays to pride.

Those gentle hours that plenty bade to bloom,
Those calm desires that asked but little room,
Those healthful sports that graced the peaceful scene,
Lived in each look, and brightened all the green;
These, far departing, seek a kinder shore,
And rural mirth and manners are no more.

 Sweet Auburn! parent of the blissful hour,
Thy glades forlorn confess the tyrant's power.
Here, as I take my solitary rounds,
Amidst thy tangling walks, and ruined grounds,

And, many a year elapsed, return to view
Where once the cottage stood, the hawthorn grew,
Remembrance wakes with all her busy train,
Swells at my breast, and turns the past to pain.

In all my wanderings round this world of care,
In all my griefs,—and God has given my share—
I still had hopes my latest hours to crown,
Amidst these humble bowers to lay me down ;
To husband out life's taper at the close,
And keep the flame from wasting by repose ;
I still had hopes, for pride attends us still,
Amidst the swains to show my book-learned skill,
Around my fire an evening group to draw,
And tell of all I felt, and all I saw ;
And, as a hare whom hounds and horns pursue,
Pants to the place from whence at first he flew,
I still had hopes, my long vexations past,
Here to return—and die at home at last.

O blest retirement, friend to life's decline,
Retreats from care, that never must be mine,
How blest is he who crowns in shades like these,
A youth of labor with an age of ease ;
Who quits a world where strong temptations try,
And, since 'tis hard to combat, learns to fly !
For him no wretches, born to work and weep,
Explore the mine, or tempt the dangerous deep ;

No surly porter stands in guilty state,
To spurn imploring famine from the gate ;
But on he moves to meet his latter end,
Angels around befriending Virtue's friend ;
Sinks to the grave with unperceived decay,
While resignation gently slopes the way ;
And, all his prospects brightening to the last,
His heaven commences ere the world be past.

Sweet was the sound, when oft, at evening's close,
Up yonder hill the village murmur rose ;
There, as I passed with careless steps and slow,
The mingling notes came softened from below ;
The swain responsive as the milk-maid sung,
The sober herd that lowed to meet their young ;
The noisy geese that gabbled o'er the pool,
The playful children just let loose from school ;
The watch-dog's voice that bayed the whispering wind;
And the loud laugh that spoke the vacant mind ;
These all in sweet confusion sought the shade,
And filled each pause the nightingale had made.
But now the sounds of population fail,
No cheerful murmurs fluctuate in the gale,
No busy steps the grass-grown foot-way tread,
But all the bloomy flush of life is fled.
All but yon widowed, solitary thing,

That feebly bends beside the plashy spring ;
She, wretched matron, forced in age, for bread,
To strip the brook with mantling cresses spread,
To pick her wintry fagot from the thorn,
To seek her nightly shed, and weep till morn ;
She only left of all the harmless train,
The sad historian of the pensive plain.

Near yonder copse, where once the garden smiled,
And still where many a garden flower grows wild ;
There, where a few torn shrubs the place disclose,
The village preacher's modest mansion rose.
A man he was to all the country dear,
And passing rich with forty pounds a year ;
Remote from towns he ran his godly race,
Nor e'er had changed, nor wished to change his place ;
Unskillful he to fawn, or seek for power,
By doctrines fashioned to the varying hour ;
Far other aims his heart had learned to prize,
More bent to raise the wretched than to rise.
His house was known to all the vagrant train,
He chid their wanderings, but relieved their pain;
The long-remembered beggar was his guest,
Whose beard descending swept his aged breast.
The ruined spendthrift, now no longer proud,
Claimed kindred there, and had his claims allowed,

The broken soldier, kindly bade to stay,
Sate by his fire, and talked the night away ;

Wept o'er his wounds, or tales of sorrow done,
Shouldered his crutch, and showed how fields were won.
Pleased with his guests, the good man learned to glow ;
And quite forgot their vices in their woe ;
Careless their merits or their faults to scan,
His pity gave ere charity began.

Thus to relieve the wretched was his pride,
And e'en his failings leaned to Virtue's side :
But in his duty prompt at every call,
He watched and wept, he prayed and felt for all ;

And, as a bird each fond endearment tries,
To tempt its new-fledged offspring to the skies,
He tried each art, reproved each dull delay,
Allured to brighter worlds, and led the way.

Beside the bed where parting life was laid,
And sorrow, guilt, and pain by turns dismayed,
The reverend champion stood.   At his control
Despair and anguish fled the struggling soul ;
Comfort came down the trembling wretch to **raise,**
And his last faltering accents whispered praise.

At church, with meek and unaffected grace,
His looks adorned the venerable place ;
Truth from his lips prevailed with double sway,
And fools, who came to scoff, remained to **pray.**
The service past, around the pious man,
With steady zeal, each honest rustic ran ;
E'en children followed with endearing wile,
And plucked his gown, to share the good man's smile.
His ready smile a parent's warmth expressed,
Their welfare pleased him, and their cares distressed,
To them his heart, his love, his griefs were given,
But all his serious thoughts had rest in heaven.
As some tall cliff that lifts its awful form,
Swells from the vale, and midway leaves the storm,
Though round its breast the rolling clouds are spread,
Eternal sunshine settles on its head.

Beside yon straggling fence that skirts the way,
With blossomed furze unprofitably gay,

There, in his noisy mansion, skilled to rule,
The village master taught his little school ;
A man severe he was, and stern to view,
I knew him well, and every truant knew ;
Well had the boding tremblers learned to trace
The day's disasters in his morning face ;
Full well they laughed with counterfeited glee
At all his jokes, for many a joke had he ;
Full well the busy whisper circling round
Conveyed the dismal tidings when he frowned ;
Yet he was kind, or if severe in aught,
The love he bore to learning was in fault ;
The village all declared how much he knew ;
'Twas certain he could write, and cipher too :
Lands he could measure, terms and tides presage,
And e'en the story ran that he could guage ;

In arguing, too, the parson owned his skill,
For e'en though vanquished, he could argue still ;
While words of learned length, and thundering sound,
Amazed the gazing rustics ranged around ;
And still they gazed, and still the wonder grew,
That one small head could carry all he knew.
    But past is all his fame. The very spot
Where many a time he triumphed, is forgot.
Near yonder thorn, that lifts its head on high,
Where once the sign-post caught the passing eye,
Low lies that house where nut-brown drafts inspired,
Where gray-beard mirth, and smiling toil retired,
Where village statesmen talked with looks profound,
And news much older than their ale went round.
Imagination fondly stoops to trace
The parlor splendors of that festive place ;
The whitewashed wall, the nicely sanded floor,
The varnished clock that clicked behind the door;
The chest contrived a double debt to pay,
A bed by night, a chest of drawers by day;
The pictures placed for ornament and use,
The twelve good rules, the royal game of goose ;
The hearth, except when winter chilled the day,
With aspen boughs, and flowers and fennel gay,
While broken tea-cups, wisely kept for show,
Ranged o'er the chimney, glistened in a row.

As some fair female unadorned and plain,
Secure to please while youth confirms her reign,
But when those charms are past, for charms are frail,
When time advances, and when lovers fail,
She then shines forth, solicitous to bless,
In all the glaring impotence of dress.
Thus fares the land by luxury betrayed,
In nature's simplest charms at first arrayed,
But verging to decline, its splendors rise,
Its vistas strike, its palaces surprise:
While, scourged by famine from the smiling land,
The mournful peasant leads his humble band;
And while he sinks, without one arm to save,
The country blooms,—a garden and a grave.

  Where, then, ah! where shall poverty reside,
To 'scape the pressure of contiguous pride?
If to some common's fenceless limits strayed
He drives his flock to pick the scanty blade,
Those fenceless fields the sons of wealth divide,
And e'en the bare-worn common is denied.

  If to the city sped,—what waits him there?
To see profusion that he must not share;
To see ten thousand baneful arts combined
To pamper luxury, and thin mankind;
To see each joy the sons of pleasure know
Extorted from his fellow-creature's woe.
Here, while the courtier glitters in brocade,

There the pale artist plies the sickly trade:
Here, while the proud their long-drawn pomps display,
There the black gibbet glooms beside the way.
The dome where Pleasure holds her midnight reign,
Here, richly decked, admits the gorgeous train:
Tumultuous grandeur crowds the blazing square,
The rattling chariots clash, the torches glare.
Sure scenes like these no troubles e'er annoy!
Sure these denote one universal joy!
Are these thy serious thoughts? Ah, turn thine eyes,
Where the poor houseless, shivering female lies.
She once, perhaps, in village plenty blest,
Has wept at tales of innocence distrest:
Her modest looks the cottage might adorn,
Sweet as the primrose peeps beneath the thorn,
Now lost to all: her friends, her virtue fled,
Near her betrayer's door she lays her head,
And, pinched with cold, and shrinking from the shower,
With heavy heart deplores that luckless hour,
When idly first, ambitious of the town,
She left her wheel and robes of country brown.
    Do thine, sweet AUBURN, thine, the loveliest train,
Do thy fair tribes participate her pain?
E'en now, perhaps, by cold and hunger led,
At proud men's doors they ask a little bread!
    Ah! no. To distant climes, a dreary scene,
Where half the convex world intrudes between,

Through torrid tracks with fainting steps they go,
Where wild Altama murmurs to their woe.
Far different there from all that charmed before,
The various terrors of that horrid shore:
Those blazing suns that dart a downward ray,
And fiercely shed intolerable day;
Those matted woods where birds forget to sing,
But silent bats in drowsy clusters cling;
Where at each step the stranger fears to wake
The rattling terrors of the vengeful snake;
Where crouching tigers wait their hapless prey,
And savage men more murderous still than they;
While oft in whirls the mad tornado flies,
Mingling the ravaged landscape with the skies.

Far different these from every former scene,
The cooling brook, the grassy vested green.

The breezy covert of the warbling grove,
That only sheltered thefts of harmless love.
Good heavens! what sorrows gloomed that parting day,
That called them from their native walks away ;
When the poor exiles, every pleasure past,
Hung round the bowers, and fondly looked their last,
And took a long farewell, and wished in vain
For seats like these beyond the western main ;
And shuddering still to face the distant deep,
Returned and wept, and still returned to weep.
The good old sire, the first prepared to go
To new-found worlds, and wept for others' woe ;
But for himself in conscious virtue brave,
He only wished for worlds beyond the grave.
His lovely daughter, lovelier in her tears,
The fond companion of his helpless years,
Silent went next, neglectful of her charms,
And left a lover's for her father's arms,
With louder plaints the mother spoke her woes,
And blessed the cot where every pleasure rose ;
And kissed her thoughtless babes with many a tear,
And clasped them close, in sorrow doubly dear ;
While her fond husband strove to lend relief
In all the silent manliness of grief.

　　　O luxury ! thou curst by heaven's decree,
How ill-exchanged are things like these for thee !
How do thy potions with insidious joy,

Diffuse their pleasures only to destroy !
Kingdoms by thee, to sickly greatness grown,
Boast of a florid vigor not their own.
At every draught more large and large they grow,
A bloated mass of rank unwieldly woe ;
Till sapped their strength, and every part unsound,
Down, down they sink, and spread a ruin round
  E'en now the devastation is begun,
And half the business of destruction done ;
E'en now, methinks, as pondering here I stand,
I see the rural virtues leave the land.
Down where yon anchoring vessel spreads the sail,
That idly waiting flaps with every gale,
Downward they move, a melancholy band,
Pass from the shore, and darken all the strand.
Contented toil and hospitable care,
And kind connubial tenderness are there ;
And piety, with wishes placed above,
And steady loyalty, and faithful love.
  And thou, sweet Poetry, thou loveliest maid,
Still first to fly where sensual joys invade ;
Unfit in these degenerate times of shame,
To catch the heart, or strike for honest fame ;
Dear charming nymph, neglected and decried,
My shame in crowds, my solitary pride,
Thou source of all my bliss, and all my woe,

That foundest me poor at first, and keepst me so ;
Thou guide by which the noble arts excel,
Thou nurse of every virtue, fare thee well !
Farewell, and O ! where'er thy voice be tried,
On Torno's cliffs, or Pambamarca's side,
Whether where equinoctial fervors glow,
Or winter wraps the polar world in snow,
Still let thy voice, prevailing over time,
Redress the rigors of the inclement clime :
Aid slighted truth with thy persuasive strain ;
Teach erring man to spurn the rage of gain ,
Teach him, that states of native strength possest,
Though very poor, may still be very blest ;
That trade's proud empire hastes to swift decay,
As ocean sweeps the labored mole away ;
While self-dependent power can time defy,
As rocks resist the billows and the sky.